GOODBYE DAISY

Written by Stephanie Nimmo

Illustrated by Helen Braid

This edition published in Great Britain by Hashtag Press 2018
Text copyright © Stephanie Nimmo 2018
Copyright Illustrations © Helen Braid 2018
Copyright Cover Design © Helen Braid 2018

A CIP catalogue for this book is available from the British Library

ISBN 978-1-9998053-7-1

Typeset in Helvetica Neue 10/13/14/15/16/20 by Helen Braid

Printed in Poland by L&C Printing Group

HASHTAG PRESS BOOKS
Hashtag Press Ltd
Kent, England, United Kingdom
Email: info@hashtagpress.co.uk
Website: www.hashtagpress.co.uk
Twitter: @hashtag_press

To my beautiful Daisy Rose
Dancing in the stars with Daddy

Elsie loved to go to school. She loved to play with all her friends.
Most of all, she loved to play with her friend Daisy.

Every day she waited at the classroom door for Daisy to arrive.

There was Lennon, racing along the corridor with his helper pushing his chair.
Little Effie followed close behind and Stevie was helping to push her chair today.

At last, Daisy arrived. Daisy was able to wheel her own chair
and Elsie could hear her friend laughing, as she whizzed along the corridor.

Elsie and Daisy hugged each other. They were best friends!

They had such fun together in school.

Playing with the toy cars in the sandpit.

Trying on silly hats.

Banging the big drum.

Looking at the books in the library.

Making handprints with the paints.

Sometimes Daisy was not in school.

Elsie knew that sometimes Daisy was poorly and she would not be able to come to school.
Sometimes, Daisy had to stay in the hospital and the doctors and nurses would look after her.

Elsie missed Daisy when she wasn't in school.

Once, when Daisy was in hospital, Elsie and her teacher, Miss Katie, made
a special 'get well' card for her. They made sure it had LOTS of glitter on it.

Daisy loved glitter.

When Daisy came back to school, Elsie was happy.
They hugged each other and played with their friends.

One day, Daisy wasn't in school. Elsie waited by the classroom door for a long time but Daisy didn't come.

She's probably got poorly again, thought Elsie. *I hope she's back in school soon.*

All the grown-ups looked sad. Some of them were crying. They were very quiet.

"I have some sad news to tell you," said Miss Katie. "We are not going to see Daisy anymore."

The children were very quiet.

Elsie wondered why they would not see Daisy. *Was she in hospital?*
Was she going to another school? Why didn't she say goodbye?

"Sadly, Daisy was poorly and this time the doctors and nurses could not make her better,"
said Miss Katie. "Sadly, Daisy has died."

What is died? thought Elsie.

Some of the children started to cry.

Elsie didn't want to cry. Elsie wanted to hide under her big scarf. She was confused.
Daisy was her best friend. Why didn't she come and say goodbye?

"Sometimes, when we are sad it makes us feel better to cry," said Miss Katie.

Elsie felt cross.

"Sometimes, when someone we love very much has died, it helps to think about all of the
happy things we did with them and that can also help us feel better," said Miss Katie.
"We won't see Daisy ever again, but we can remember all the happy times we had with her."

Miss Katie got the big box of art and craft supplies from the cupboard so
the children could draw pictures of their happy memories with Daisy.

Elsie didn't want to think about the happy things she did with Daisy. Elsie folded her arms;
she was confused and cross and she certainly did not want to draw pictures!

She pushed the box of colouring pencils across the table and the tub of glitter fell onto the floor.

"Oh Elsie!" said Miss Katie. "Why did you do that? Now there's glitter everywhere."

Why didn't Daisy say goodbye? Elsie thought to herself. *She was my best friend.*

Later that evening, Elsie was at home. She sat on the sofa.
Elsie put her scarf over her head and folded her arms.

She didn't want to watch TV.

She didn't want to eat her favourite custard cream biscuits.

She didn't want to play with her big brother.

She was cross with Daisy. She was her best friend, so why hadn't she said goodbye?

There was a knock at the door. Elsie's Mum opened it.

It was Daisy's Mummy.

Daisy's Mummy looked sad, her eyes were red and she was crying.
Elsie's Mummy began to cry. They hugged each other.

They hugged Elsie. Elsie felt confused. She wanted to know why her friend had not said goodbye.

Elsie had so many questions and no-one was listening.

Daisy's Mummy spoke to Elsie.

"Every night when Daisy went to bed I would put on her special nightlight," she said. "Daisy
loved her nightlight because it lit up her bedroom with lots of stars and this made her happy.
I told Daisy that the stars were like glitter in the sky! I want you to have Daisy's special light now."

If she has gone away, why hasn't she taken her special nightlight? thought Elsie.

When it was bedtime, Elsie's Mummy switched on Daisy's special night light. It filled the ceiling with stars.

"Goodnight Elsie," said her Mummy.

Elsie looked up at the stars on her ceiling. *Glitter in the sky*, she thought to herself.
Elsie's eyelids felt heavy and she fell asleep.

As she slept she started to dream about her friend.

Suddenly, she heard a voice very quietly calling her name, "Elsie, Elsie..."
The voice was getting louder, it was laughing…

"Elsie, Elsie! Elsie, it's me - Daisy!"

Elsie sat up.

"Daisy!" she called out. "Where are you?"

"Look up Elsie, I'm in the stars!"

Elsie looked up at the stars on her ceiling, there was Daisy!
She was laughing and waving.

Elsie waved back.

"Daisy," called Elsie. "Why did you go away? Miss Katie says I won't see you anymore."

"I'm sorry I couldn't say goodbye," said Daisy. "I was poorly and tired and the doctors couldn't fix me."

"But you didn't take your things… you left your special light," said Elsie.

"I don't need it, it's yours now," said Daisy. "I want you to have it, so that when you feel sad you can look at the stars and think of me dancing and playing. You can remember all the happy times we spent together. I will always be your friend, Elsie, and I will never forget you."

"I love you Daisy," called Elsie.

"I love you Elsie," laughed Daisy, as she danced across the sky.

Big tears rolled down Elsie's cheeks. She felt sad.

Then she remembered all the things she and Daisy had done together.

When they had played with the toy cars in the sandpit.

When they had tried on silly hats.

When they had banged the big drum.

When they had looked at books in the library.

When they had made handprints with the paints.

Elsie smiled. She still felt sad, but she did not feel so cross any more. Thinking about all of the happy times she had spent with Daisy made her feel happy inside.

The next day Elsie went back to school.

"Would you like to make something special to remember Daisy?" asked Miss Katie.

Elsie knew what do.

Together, Elsie and Miss Katie made a big star, they painted it silver and covered it in lots of glitter.

Daisy LOVED glitter. It was Daisy's star.

Together, Miss Katie and Elsie went out into the garden and they hung Daisy's star on a tree.

She thought of her friend dancing in the stars.

Elsie smiled.

"Goodbye Daisy," she said.

Daisy's story

by her Mummy

My little girl, Daisy, was born in December 2004. She was my fourth child. She arrived into our lives two months earlier than planned. Not long afterwards, we were told that she had a very rare genetic condition and was unlikely to reach adulthood.

I gave up work to become Daisy's full time carer, nurse, advocate and Mummy. The doctors couldn't tell us what Daisy's life expectancy was, in fact, at that point, they were not even sure if she would see her first birthday.

Daisy was a feisty, determined, little girl and despite bouncing in and out of hospital, and ever-increasing complications with her health, she defied the odds. Not only did she get to celebrate her first birthday, a few years later I was the proudest mum in town when I took Daisy to school for the first time.

Daisy loved school! And everyone in her school loved Daisy. She was a larger than life character, with a mop of blond curls and an infectious smile. When she lost the ability to walk, we bought her a wheelchair. She loved to whizz along the school corridors in it.

Daisy had a big circle of friends, she loved her friends! School was about socialising and playing and fun, as far as Daisy was concerned.

Daisy had many hospital stays, often for months at a time. During this time, she would attend the hospital school or her support assistant would come to the hospital and bring along Daisy's "busy work" from her teacher. Sometimes, we would even Skype her school friends so that she could still feel part of the class and they could all see her.

We knew from very early on that Daisy would not be with us forever, that she would likely not reach adulthood. Living with that knowledge made us very determined to enjoy every moment of our precious time with our girl. Despite her learning disability and minimal verbal skills, Daisy was very clear about what she wanted in life. Her most important priorities were spending time at home with her siblings and her beloved dog Pluto, shopping (that girl loved to shop!) and going to school to see her friends.

Daisy had many, many hospital stays in her short life, but her determination and grit meant that even after coming through yet another episode of sepsis, her first thoughts would be about when she could get back home and then to school to see her friends. While we were embracing every day - enjoying precious time with Daisy during her stable periods - our family was hit with a huge bombshell. Daisy's Daddy, my husband Andy, was diagnosed with stage four, incurable bowel cancer. We were devastated, but soon realised that life with Daisy had taught us to live in the moment. We were already doing this, now we were more determined than ever to make the most of our finite time.

My biggest concern was how to break the news to our children and how to support them through Andy's illness and inevitable death. We had always chosen to be very honest with our older three. They were seven, five and two when Daisy was born. When we were referred to a children's hospice a few months later, for ongoing support and respite, they understood that it was because Daisy was expected to have a shorter life than other children (although we emphasised her death was not imminent). We were as honest with the children about Andy's diagnosis, we reassured them that his death was not imminent, but that his cancer was not curable, so it was more important than ever to make sure we really savoured the time we had together.

When it came to Daisy I was very concerned. I did not want her to think that whatever happened to Andy would also happen to her. Like many children with learning disabilities, her receptive skills were far in advance of her ability to communicate. In other words, she understood a lot more than she could tell us. I told her that Daddy had a special poorly and that he too would need a wiggly (the word we used for the Hickman line that Daisy had inserted into a main vein in her chest through which she received all of her nutrition).

She thought it was hilarious that Daddy was now the patient and clearly understood that he was unwell.

I took advice from a good friend of mine in the blogging community who had been living long term with stage four breast cancer. Her son was older than Daisy and lived in a group home but one thing she told me struck home: do not hide Andy's symptoms from Daisy, she needs to see his deterioration for herself.

As Andy grew close to end of life I did not use upbeat words like "getting better," rather I let Daisy see Andy when he was at home and quite obviously deteriorating.

Daisy was staying in her children's hospice when Andy died. I went into her room to break the news to her, getting into her bed to tell her. She knew why I was there and signed the Makaton sign for sad. I used the word died, I told her that we would not see Daddy any more but that he loved her very much and he would want her to think about all of the happy things we did together.

With school and the hospice we made pictures and a memory box. We put lots of pictures of Andy and the family in the memory box, so that Daisy could look at them whenever she wanted. We used the pictures to talk about Andy. Daisy wanted to talk about Andy every day. Anyone who came to the house was told, "Goodbye Daddy" and shown the sign for sad.

Daisy's school also made a wonderful social story about Andy for Daisy. It explained that Daddy had a special poorly and the doctors couldn't make him better but that it was important to remember all the happy things that Daisy had done with Andy. Daisy got huge comfort from this book and it was carried with her everywhere for the next thirteen months of her life.

Andy's death coincided with a rapid deterioration in Daisy's health. It had been in sharp decline for a while but the grief at the loss of her beloved Daddy seemed to speed up her physical demise and affected her ability to fight back from infections.

In January 2017, Daisy was transferred to Great Ormond Street hospital from our local hospital. This was not an unfamiliar routine for us but this time I felt that Daisy was not bouncing back as she normally did. She was overwhelmed with sepsis and went into irreversible organ failure. On the 31st January 2017, I made the decision to switch off Daisy's ventilator and I told her to go and dance in the stars with her Daddy.

We were heartbroken. Yet, I soon realised that it was not just us, her family, who were heartbroken, it takes a village to raise a child with complex needs. So many people were involved in Daisy's life and they were all mourning her loss. None more than her little friends in school.

I remember going to visit a close friend one evening, not long after Daisy had died. Her daughter, one of Daisy's school-friends and also non-verbal, was trying to communicate with me, "Where is Daisy? Why isn't she in school?" her eyes asked me.

It struck me that while we adults could talk and mourn and cry, the children in Daisy's school were struggling to articulate and understand their grief at the loss of their friend. Daisy's school were amazing. Daisy had been a pupil there from the age of three - everyone knew her - so the impact of her death was felt across the entire school. A few days after she died, the school community gathered in the playground and the head teacher talked about Daisy. The children then released pink balloons and played some of Daisy's favourite music.

The teaching staff made a social story to be used in class discussions about Daisy. This explained in very simple but direct terms that Daisy had been poorly and the children would not see her any more as she had died. There were lots of pictures of the fun things that Daisy had got up to in school so that the class could look at them and have happy memories of their time with her.

I visited some of Daisy's special friends and gave them a gift. A toy, a blanket, a cushion that had once belonged to Daisy, together with a copy of the social story, so that they could look at pictures of their friend.

When it came to Daisy's funeral I knew I had to involve the school in some way. I needed the funeral to be a community event so that everyone could gain some comfort in saying goodbye. We held her funeral in the school hall (fortunately it was half term) and involved nurses, carers, doctors and teachers in the service. There was music and laughter and sadness. Many of the children from school came along, one little girl said it was a party for Daisy. When the hearse drove away with Daisy's little pink, willow coffin, a rainbow appeared over the school. I had asked everyone to come to the funeral wearing bright colours so that we could create a rainbow in Daisy's memory. When I saw the rainbow appear I felt that Daisy was thanking us and telling us it would be alright, just as she does with Elsie in this book.

You may be reading this book because you are the parent or carer of a child who has lost a friend, or will face the loss of a friend. Every situation is different, but this is what worked for me, I hope it helps:

Be open and honest.

For the child to be able to work through their grief they need to know it's OK to grieve, you can show them that it's OK to cry; model the emotions for them.

Do not use euphemisms.

Saying things like "gone to a better place" is very confusing for any child, especially a child with learning disabilities. Try to be direct and avoid any doubt with the language you use.

Develop social stories.

Social stories help articulate the feelings of loss and grief. They don't have to be big elaborate affairs, just talking about the emotions your child is feeling is a good start.

Do not underestimate your child's grief and frustration.

Non-verbal children still feel the same emotions as verbal children. When Elsie pushes the crayons off the table, it's because she's frustrated and cannot articulate her feelings in the same way a verbal child may be able to.

Do not shy away.

Talk about the child who has gone and make sure they are remembered. Find ways to commemorate them with your child, as Elsie does with her teacher.

Reassure your child.

They may worry that they will die soon too. While there are no guarantees in life, the likelihood is this will not happen to your child, so reassure them that their friend dying does not mean that they will leave soon too.

Do not hide your own grief.

It's important to say that you feel sad too, then talk about what makes you sad and what makes you happy. When I told Daisy that her Daddy had died I told her that I was sad too. We looked at pictures on my phone of Andy making silly faces and we talked about how he made us laugh. I told her that is was OK to feel happy and sad. In our family we call it "happy-sad."

Be prepared to talk about what happened for a long time.

Daisy talked about her Daddy every day; even when I didn't want to talk about him dying she did and often when I least expected it.

For the Professionals

Stephanie's Story

We were very conscious that despite her learning disability, Daisy was very aware of the deterioration in her physical skills and this frustration often manifested in challenging behaviour. We wanted to find help to support her mental health needs but there seemed to be nothing available for a child who was non-verbal with complex health needs. We knew that although Daisy could not speak and was categorised as having profound and multiple learning disabilities she still felt grief and loss, and through our experience with our other children, we were aware that she could feel anticipatory grief at the loss of the freedom and control over her body that she had once enjoyed, even though that had been limited.

At every meeting with professionals we brought up the issue of Daisy's mental health. Our other children were receiving therapeutic support through child and adolescent mental health services, so why was Daisy's mental health being neglected?

Daisy's wonderful special needs school provided us with the breakthrough we were seeking when they proposed she began therapy sessions with Ella, a Dance Movement Psychotherapist who had a particular interest in working with children with profound learning disabilities.

Ella's involvement in Daisy's life every week made a huge difference, as it allowed her the safe and understanding space she needed to articulate her feelings about what was happening.

Ella combined play and observation to allow Daisy to communicate her innermost thoughts. Daisy's last session with Ella was exactly one week before she died, this was a very personal and private session between therapist and child and I am so grateful that Daisy had that opportunity to spend some time sharing, in a non-verbal way, her feelings. I am convinced that Daisy knew she was dying and I am grateful that she was allowed some space and peace before she slipped into unconsciousness and was put on life support.

After Daisy's death, the children in the school were aware that she had gone. Some felt confused, sad and angry and this manifested in their behaviours, as it does with Elsie in the story.

A few days after the news of her death, the whole school came together to remember Daisy. There was a balloon release with messages attached and a memory book made with comments and photos of Daisy from the staff involved in her care and education. The school staff were offered support to talk about their feelings and given the opportunity to attend counselling sessions.

I took some of Daisy's ashes back to school and we scattered them in a small garden that the staff could visit and have a quiet moment of reflection. Some of the staff who were part of Daisy's school life came along at my invitation, her teacher read out some beautiful words and we played one of Daisy's favourite songs.

As we scattered the ashes and planted a beautiful pink hydrangea in the garden, a robin appeared and watched us. It was like Daisy had sent him along to say one last goodbye.

There is also a memorial garden in Daisy's school, the Friends Forever garden. It's a place the children can visit to remember their friends, those who have moved away, those who have left school to go onto college, those who have died. I hung a star in the garden so that Daisy's special friends could go and remember her and have a focus for their grief.

Ella's Story

Once upon a time, there was a beautiful Princess called Daisy. When Princess Daisy was born, seven fairies came to see her. They gave her gifts. One of courage, one of resilience, one of a cracking sense of humour, one of intelligence, one of love, one of beauty and one of curiosity. Suddenly, there was a puff of pink smoke and Daisy's Fairy Godmother appeared to her. "Daisy," she said. "When the clock strikes twelve, you must return to the pink castle in the sky." Everyone was in disbelief, but Daisy just smiled..."

(Taken from Ella Beard's words at Daisy's funeral)

As a Dance Movement Psychotherapist, the heart of the work I do is the creation of a trusting relationship - this was my initial goal with Daisy. Once established, Daisy was able to let me enter her world and help support her emotional well-being and mental health in a non-verbal and creative way.

Daisy arrived at the Dance Movement Psychotherapy (DMP) sessions with a small rucksack full of emergency medication on the back of her wheelchair, various tubes and pumps and an ileostomy bag hanging from her tummy. She was wearing Minnie Mouse ears and was full of vitality. As soon as she entered the therapy room, she had a plan. She went straight to the Doctor's kit I had laid out and began to tell her story…

Daisy was a non-verbal child; using sounds, words and Makaton signing to communicate with those around her. She knew what she wanted to say, and it was up to us to find a way into her world to understand what she wanted us to know. In our therapy sessions, this communication was through symbolic play and body movement. Our focus was on building a trusting relationship in which Daisy could feel comfortable enough to let me understand what she was feeling, seeing and sensing.

Daisy used the sessions to play out what she was experiencing in her life - in her world. She was able to explore her feelings and share how overwhelmed and how out of control she could feel at times. The themes focused on how she was managing to live with the continuous challenges at a bodily level and emotional level.

In these sessions, Daisy was in control, which could help ease anxiety. The feelings that Daisy brought to the sessions, and left in the therapy room, supported her in being able to process her own experiences and to not be completely overwhelmed by them. She could leave them with me, move on and focus more on her school time, home time and time with friends.

At school, it was important to be able to think together with the multidisciplinary team. On one occasion, it had become apparent that Daisy was becoming very distressed and this was because she was aware of an impending surgery. Her distress was very clear in her therapy sessions. I knew that we needed to act on Daisy's anxiety.

With Steph, Daisy's teacher and a Speech and Language Therapist, we created a photo book to help Daisy and the medical team prepare her for any operations or procedures as best they could. It was full of photos of the props from our sessions, such as implements from the Doctor's kit. This gave the medical team a way to explain to Daisy what they were going to do so she could anticipate it and be prepared. This gave the medical staff a deeper understanding of how much Daisy understood and needed to understand. This book helped the channels of communication for both hospital staff and for Daisy and it seemed to help lessen her anxiety and distress before operations.

Steph and her husband, Andy, fought hard to get Daisy's DMP sessions funded and included as part of her educational support plan; this was not an easy task, but they achieved it. They knew the importance of this emotional support and outlet in allowing Daisy to be a little girl and not just a patient.

They also knew what was on the horizon for Daisy. Life was only going to get more challenging: increased loss of mobility, increased loss of control of bodily functions, increased loss of energy and more visits to hospitals and stays at hospices. Her condition was life-limiting and she was surviving even longer than anyone could have dreamed of. Steph and Andy believed that every child, even those with learning disabilities and non-verbal communication, should have the right to psychotherapeutic support to help them cope with life's challenges.

But no-one foresaw what would happen next. A challenge like no other before. When Daisy was ten, her beloved Daddy, Andy, took ill and within the year had died. Daisy was heart-broken. Steph had always been very open and honest with Daisy about what was going to happen to Andy and this transparency seemed to help Daisy process his death. Our sessions continued weekly where she had a space to grieve, be angry, sad and curious. But like many other children who lose a parent or a family member, she became concerned about the other members of her family. Would someone else take sick and die?

Daisy's DMP sessions continued right up to the week before her death. Thanks to Steph, we even managed to have a session in the hospital! Steph pulled the curtain around us and stuck my 'Please Do Not Disturb' sign to the curtain. This was our last session. This time, the session was in real-time: the medical team, the medical kit, the hospital sounds, the pain, the curiosity and the courage.

Daisy died on the 31st January 2017. She was twelve years old. When the news came through, the whole school was in shock. Daisy had defied the odds over and over and seemed like she would go on forever. We couldn't believe she was gone and we would not see her again. If the adults felt like that, how were the children in the school, all of whom had learning disabilities and varying language ability, coping with this news?

The head teacher took the decision to bring the whole school together to remember Daisy. Everyone gathered in the playground and a pink balloon was released and some of Daisy's favourite songs were played. Later that week, the school staff put together a memory book full of comments and photos of Daisy from all the staff involved in her care and education.

Each class was given a special social story book, which used simple language to explain that the children would not see Daisy again. It was full of pictures of her happy times spent at school - for the children to look at and for the class to discuss. Daisy's close friends were given their own copy of the social story to take home with them. After Daisy died, I worked with her class and through group dance movement psychotherapy sessions, gave Daisy's close friends space to process their loss in a non-verbal way and creative way.

The whole school community was affected by Daisy's death. She was such a resilient, feisty and larger than life character who had joined the school at the age of three and had certainly made her mark on everyone; the teaching staff, support staff, travel escorts, even the school reception team knew Daisy well!

Death and Bereavement in SEN schools

Advice on what to do when a child dies in a school community

Staff play a vital role in supporting young people when faced with the death of a friend or peer. They might also be affected by their own losses and this must be taken into consideration when supporting them.

Some schools have counsellors who can provide sessions in-house or via external organisations and charities. Where possible, it is helpful to provide small-group or individual support in school in the form of weekly de-brief sessions/counselling, giving staff support very soon after the actual death. This allows staff time to be heard and supported within the school's working day.

Every school should have its own Bereavement Policy. This acts as a framework and is not set in stone given that the area of loss is emotive, and the Policy needs to be sensitive to each unique situation, the young person and their family. It should also be regularly reviewed. This response from the school should be sensitive to the family's wishes and respectful to the cultural and religious background of each family. It is important that the family of the deceased be consulted about the school's response. However, the school also has a responsibility to its other children, young people and staff and need to find ways of providing support and time to grieve and remember. Some ideas might be:

A balloon release with messages attached (at Daisy's funeral Steph released two doves, one for Daisy and one for Andy, her Daddy. A local undertaker can organise this as an alternative to a balloon release).

Memory book – photos and messages to give to the family.

Social stories for each class, which are appropriate to the needs of the young people.

A special assembly with photos and favourite music.

A reflective space – a garden, a table, a space that can be a focal point for conversations and discussions. Perhaps somewhere to put a memento just as Elsie hangs a star on the tree in the memory garden to remember Daisy?

An annual memory day for all the pupils who have died (with an opportunity for families to attend and feel that they remain part of the school community).

A memory garden with plaques bearing the young people's names where pupils, staff and families can visit.

Planting of a tree/a flower.

It can be difficult to get right but there are so many ways to do it well by continuing to review the policy and the support available.

The whole school community should made aware of the death of a young person and notified of any whole school events planned to celebrate their life, from the escorts involved in transport to the cleaning staff. It may be that there are also smaller, more individual ways of supporting staff and children, which might not be appropriate for the whole school to attend. It is important to ask staff and students about how they feel they would like to remember the young person, so that everyone thinks together and feels included.

It is vital to provide on-going support moving forward and not just in the immediate aftermath of the death of a child. Regular keeping-in-touch sessions with staff are extremely helpful in order to have a space to reflect and to get adequate support in place.

Acknowledgements

It takes a village to raise a child, especially a child with additional needs, my grateful thanks to everyone who walked our path with us during Daisy's short but oh so wonderful time on earth.

This book would not have been possible without the generosity of the many people who pledged vital funds and helped to spread the word.

My grateful thanks especially go to the following pledgers:

The Hadman family in loving memory of our beautiful Effie

Stevie and the Lawrence Family

The Best Family

Rosa Monckton and Team Domenica

Richard, Marion, Daniel, Amy and Hannah Germain

Anonymous donor "To our much loved Nanny Val on your special birthday"

To Focused Healthcare for your very generous donation.

To my publishers Hashtag Press for your faith in me and for putting up with my constantly changing goalposts.

To Helen Braid - for your uncanny knack of seeing into my head and turning my vision into the most beautiful illustrations.

To Ella - for giving Daisy her voice and space to be heard.

To Sue Curtis DMP - for your professional feedback and advice.

To Daisy's friends who taught me so much.

Remembering all the little stars…

Effie, Lennon, Oliver, Rhys, Maddie, Alicia, Melody, Brodie, Rocco, Abigail, Clayton, Kenzie, Quinn, Willa, Zachary, Bret, Nicola… and all the children whose stay on earth was short. RIP.

Lastly, to Daisy's brothers and sister, Theo, Xanthe and Jules.
Your strength and courage in the face of all that life has thrown is incredible.
Go out into the world and be amazing xxx

About the author

Steph is a vocal campaigner and advocate for engaging people in difficult conversations around death and dying. Her first book, Was This in the Plan? charts her own experience of the death of her husband from terminal cancer. Although she was born and raised in Wales, Steph has called London her home since 1990. She lives in Wimbledon with her three older children and is on an ongoing mission to continually embarrass them by always dancing like no-one is watching.

www.StephNimmo.com

About the therapist

Ella is a Registered Dance Movement Psychotherapist (RDMP) and part of the Creative and Therapeutic Arts Team at the Special Needs school attended by Daisy. She works with children and young people with Profound and Multiple Learning Disabilities (PMLD) and Multi-Sensory Impairments (MSI), supporting groups and individuals to explore ways of exploring feelings and communicating in a safe space, using verbal and non-verbal communication. Ella is a member of the ADMPUK (Association of Dance Movement Psychotherapy UK.

About the illustrator

Helen Braid lives on the beautiful Northumberland coast which is a constant source of inspiration for her illustrations. Helen first met Stephanie when she was commissioned to produce the artwork for her blog. She works from her cottage studio surrounded by pens, watercolours, and cups of cappuccino.

www.ellieillustrates.co.uk

For resources and information on how to
support a child with learning disabilities
when one of their friends dies go to
www.GoodbyeDaisy.com

Daisy Rose Nimmo

Sunrise 22 December 2004
Sunset 31 January 2017